E
Smi

Smith, Barry
    Minnie and Ginger

DATE DUE			
9-13			
4-1			
4-30			
8/15			
12/31			

Easter

Thanks to RTB for help, encouragement and advice.

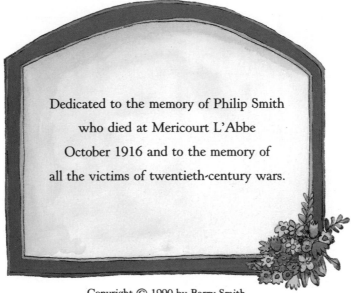

Dedicated to the memory of Philip Smith
who died at Mericourt L'Abbe
October 1916 and to the memory of
all the victims of twentieth-century wars.

Published by Clarkson N. Potter, Inc., a Random House Company
201 East 50th Street, New York, NY 10022.

Originally published in Great Britain by Pavilion Books Limited
in 1990.

CLARKSON N. POTTER, POTTER, and colophon are trademarks
of Clarkson N. Potter, Inc.

Manufactured in Great Britain

Library of Congress in Publication Data is available on request.
Library of Congress Catalog Card Number: 90–40330.

ISBN 0–517–58253–8

10 9 8 7 6 5 4 3 2 1

First American Edition

Minnie Hardcastle lived with her mother, father, three sisters and two brothers at
16 Railway Terrace.

Ginger Earnshaw lived at 18 with his mother, father, four brothers, a sister, two uncles, a grandmother, a cat and a parrot called Nettie.

Minnie and Ginger liked each other.
They had finished school and now were going to work
to help their families.

Ginger found a job in Jervis
Robinson's soap factory.

Minnie found a job as an assistant milliner at Myrtle Walker's hat and glove shop.

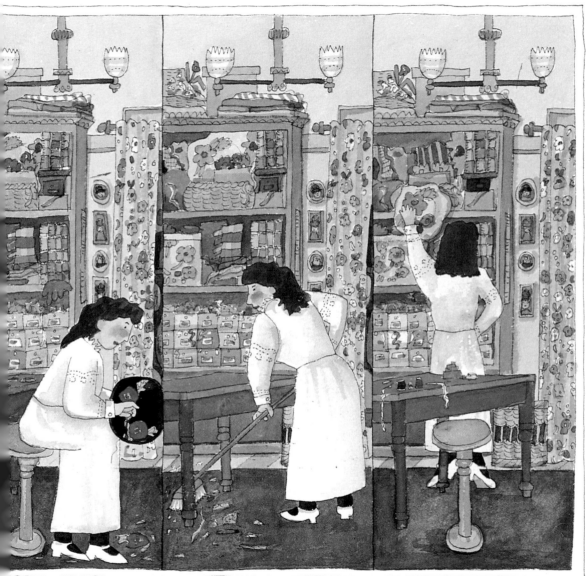

Ginger worked hard at the factory.
Minnie worked hard, too.

But Minnie and Ginger enjoyed themselves on picnics, at parties,

at fairs and on outings to the sea.

Ginger played football; Minnie went cycling.

Best of all, they enjoyed being alone on Sunday evenings, although they were
never alone for long.

Minnie and Ginger decided to get married. All Ginger's family came to the wedding and all Minnie's family came to the wedding.

Everyone had a grand time – even Ginger's grandmother in a new hat trimmed
with red poppies that Minnie had made.

Minnie and Ginger settled into their own home near Mr Herbert's piano factory.

After a time,
Minnie and Ginger had a baby.

And another. Soon there were four children.

But one day something dreadful happened. War was declared. A terrible war.

Ginger had to leave his four
children, leave Minnie
and his home and fight
in that war.

Ginger was in the army, far away from home in the Great War, as it was called.

Ginger was so frightened.

Minnie and the four children were frightened too.
Ginger was away for a long time!

Finally, the Great War came to an end.

Ginger came home to Minnie
and his four children.

Minnie and Ginger lived
quite happily together

with only the occasional
disagreement

for quite a long time.